D1608882

Words to Know Before You Read

half

hungry

other

pizza

share

whole

www.rourkeeducationalmedia.com

Edited by Precious McKenzie
Illustrated by Helen Poole
Art Direction and Page Layout by Renee Brady

Library of Congress PCN Data

Let's Get Pizza / Meg Greve
ISBN 978-1-61810-173-0 (hard cover) (alk. paper)
ISBN 978-1-61810-306-2 (soft cover)
Library of Congress Control Number: 2012936774

Rourke Educational Media
Printed in the United States of America,
North Mankato, Minnesota

rourkeeducationalmedia.com

customerservice@rourkeeducationalmedia.com • PO Box 643328 Vero Beach, Florida 32964

Let's Get Pizza

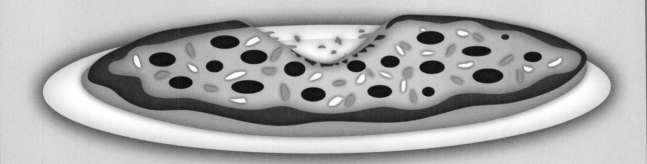

By Meg Greve

Illustrated by Helen Poole

Dan and Dad want pizza. Dan wants to get the pizza.

Tasty!

yum!

Mmm!

5

The pizza smells really good.
Dan is VERY hungry. He eats half
on the way back to the booth.

He eats the other half too!

9

"You ate the WHOLE thing!"
says Dad.

Dad wants to get more pizza.

Tasty!

12

13

The pizza smells really good.
Dad is VERY hungry. He eats half
on the way back to the booth.

Tasty!

He eats the other half too!

"You ate the WHOLE thing!"
says Dan.

"Let's get more pizza," says Dad.
"We'll each eat half!" says Dan.

Tasty!

After Reading Activities

You and the Story...

Why did Dan eat the whole pizza?

How many halves make a whole?

What could you do if there were four people and only one pizza?

How would you share?

Words You Know Now...

Write three words from the list below on a piece of paper.
Write a word that rhymes with each of the words. Now write a
sentence including the original word and the rhyming word.

half	pizza
hungry	share
other	whole

You Could...Make a Pizza!

Make a simple pizza with an adult's help.

You Will Need:
    One English muffin
    Pizza sauce
    Cheese
    Cut up vegetables

Steps:
1. Take half of an English muffin and spread pizza sauce on it.
2. Sprinkle cheese and your favorite vegetables on top.
3. Broil it in the oven until the cheese is bubbly and hot.
4. Make the other half and share it with a friend!

About the Author

Meg Greve lives in Chicago with her husband, daughter, and son. They love to eat gooey, cheesy, hot pizza!

Ask The Author!
www.rem4students.com

About the Illustrator

Helen Poole lives in Liverpool, England, with her fiancé. Over the past ten years she has worked as a designer and illustrator on books, toys, and games for many stores and publishers worldwide. Her favorite part of illustrating is character development. She loves creating fun, whimsical worlds with bright, vibrant colors. She gets her inspiration from everyday life and has her sketchbook with her at all times as inspiration often strikes in the unlikeliest of places!